www.hmhbooks.com

Houghton Mifflin Books for Children is an imprint
of Houghton Mifflin Harcourt Publishing Company.

The text of this book is set in Clichee.
The illustrations in this book are mixed media, acrylic, collage . . . and whimsy.

Library of Congress Cataloging-in-Publication Data
Noyes, Deborah.
    Prudence and Moxie A Tale of Mismatched Friends /
    by Deborah Noyes; illustrated by AnnaLaura Cantone.
      p. cm.
    Summary: Timid, quiet Prudence is surprised to learn that her
    very loud and very brave friend Moxie is afraid of horses.
    ISBN-13: 978-0-618-41607-3
    [1. Friendship—Fiction. 2. Courage—Fiction. 3. Fear—Fiction.]
    I. Cantone, Anna-Laura, ill. II. Title.
      PZ7.N96157Pr 2008
      [E]—dc22   2007025778

Printed in Singapore
TWP 10 9 8 7 6 5 4 3 2 1

Prudence & Moxie

A Tale of Mismatched Friends

By Deborah Noyes   Illustrated by AnnaLaura Cantone

Houghton Mifflin Books for Children

HOUGHTON MIFFLIN HARCOURT • BOSTON 2009

When Prudence and Moxie and their class visit the aquarium, Charlie Hardy says, "I dare you," and Moxie makes kissy faces at sharks. Her nose squishes flat as rays ripple past.

Moxie must look funny to the fish, thinks Prudence.

When Prudence and Moxie go sledding on High Horse Hill,
Prudence imagines they are prisoners in the carriage of the Snow Queen.

"Dare you!" shouts Pablo, and Moxie rolls off the sled, over and down, round and round, till she loses her mittens.

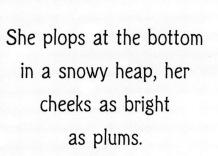

She plops at the bottom in a snowy heap, her cheeks as bright as plums.

Prudence hurries to fetch the
sled and trudges back up High
Horse Hill. Sometimes she wishes
Moxie had never moved into the
little blue house next door to her
little brown house on Peach Street.

It's always the same: "I dare you, Moxie!" and "I bet you won't." *She will,* thinks Prudence. *She always does.*

Moxie spoils every game.

When Prudence and Moxie go to the movies, Moxie talks back to the screen. If the movie is a romance, she toots her nose into a tissue. If it's a Western, Moxie swish-waves an invisible lasso until the people behind her hiss, "Shhhhh."

Patient Prudence fixes her gaze on the screen while the heroine rides her pony across the plains. "Moxie," she pleads, "do you always have to be loudest?"

Moxie nods with gusto. "And fastest. And bravest."

"If you're so brave . . ."

". . . and like lassos so much," Prudence whispers,
"how come you won't come to the stables and
meet my horse?"

"I gave a horse a carrot once." Moxie shudders. "He had big teeth and bad manners, and he bit me. The doctor said I might never recover."

"My horse has perfect manners," says Prudence.

"Shhhhh." Moxie settles back with crossed arms. "*Some of us* are trying to watch the movie."

In springtime, when Prudence and Moxie and the gang visit the country fair, Moxie's brother Ned shouts, "I double dare you!" and Moxie hops up behind the wheel of a giant tractor. She rattles the gears, calling the machine her Tyrannosaurus rex.

Smiling, Moxie's dad plucks her down. They walk away to have "a quiet moment."

Prudence thinks she'll take an Appaloosa over a T. rex any day, and she will ride that horse away from too loud, too brave people who call themselves friends. Far away.

Later, when Prudence pulls Moxie toward the stables, Moxie tugs in the other direction.

And she doesn't look brave at all.

At the amusement park in August, Moxie and Sammy Spiers ride the Submarine Sling over and over.
"Again!" shouts Sammy.
"I double dog dare you."

"Over here!" Prudence is riding the little carousel—around and around. "Look at me, Moxie—" Moxie is too busy to look, too woozy to smile, though she manages a little wave.

"I triple dare you to ride Ned's high-speed turbo go-cart down High Horse Hill with no hands," Sammy whispers in the car on the way home.
Moxie says she'll think about it.

Later that week Prudence goes to Moxie's house for a cookout. Moxie eats two of everything and smacks her lips.

A storm blows over. Lightning flashes purple-white. Prudence hides as the thunder rumbles like the stomach of a hungry giant, moving away.

Moxie takes Prudence by the hand. She takes Prudence by surprise. "I love thunder," she whispers. And Prudence can see that she does.

Little by little, Moxie pulls Prudence out into the street. All the neighborhood kids are there—dancing, twirling, tasting rain. Moxie's mother brings out a watermelon.

Prudence has a smile all ready, but before Ned can say "dare," Moxie is off spitting watermelon seeds at the Newhouse twins.

"Sammy says you're scared
to ride your brother's high-speed turbo go-cart
down High Horse Hill with no hands." Nora Newhouse
plucks watermelon seeds from her fairy princess leotard.

"Scared?" bellows Moxie.

"That's right—scared. Chicken," adds Nora. "Cluck." She
flaps her arms. "Cluck. Cluck."

Moxie sticks out her chin and begins to march. Every kid
in the neighborhood marches behind her.

Prudence has a terrible, terrible feeling about this. "Oh,
no, don't! Wait! Moxie . . ."

After Moxie heals, Prudence's dad asks them to rake the yard. Mervin Millhouse peers over the fence and offers to pay Moxie a nickel if she'll do handstands and home base slides in the leaves.

"I triple dog dare you,"
Mervin adds.

Prudence quietly goes on raking in her red cowboy boots.

For a time—a longer time than usual—Moxie considers.

"Maybe I will," she announces, "and maybe I won't." And then
she looks at Prudence. "What do you think, Prudence?"

Prudence smiles.

Together, Moxie and Prudence stand with lifted chins,
waiting for Mervin to go.

When he goes, they whoop
and slide home in the leaves.

Prudence asks, "Won't you please come to the stables one
day? To meet Thunder?"
Moxie shudders.
"Please?"
"All right, Prudence. I will."

"For you."

One day Moxie *does* come to the stables, and she is very quiet. She stops at the barn door and won't budge.

Prudence gives her a nudge.
"You aren't scared, *are* you?"
Moxie digs her heels in the dirt.

"I dare you?" Prudence calls from inside, leading Thunder out of his stall.

Moxie gasps when her friend climbs up and strokes the horse's mane.

"I'll be with you." Prudence reaches down. "Right up here with you."

"Maybe I will," Moxie says in a too-big voice, "and maybe I won't."

Leaning low, Prudence whispers, "I love Thunder." And Moxie can see that she does. She takes her friend's hand. Slowly, carefully, Moxie slips her foot into the stirrup and climbs up, up behind Prudence, and holds tight.